The United States

New York

Anne Welsbacher
ABDO & Daughters

Come visit us at
www.abdopub.com

Published by Abdo & Daughters, 4940 Viking Drive, Suite 622, Edina, Minnesota 55435.
Copyright © 1998 by Abdo Consulting Group, Inc., Pentagon Tower, P.O. Box 36036, Minne-
apolis, Minnesota 55435 USA. International copyrights reserved in all countries. No part of
this book may be reproduced in any form without written permission from the publisher.

Printed in the United States.

Cover and Interior Photo credits: Peter Arnold, Inc., SuperStock, Archive, Corbis-Bettmann

Edited by Lori Kinstad Pupeza
Contributing editor: Michele M. Kelley
Special thanks to our Checkerboard Kids—Francesca Tuminelly, Raymond Sherman, Teddy
Borth

All statistics taken from the 1990 census; The Rand McNally Discovery Atlas of the United
States.

Library of Congress Cataloging-in-Publication Data

Welsbacher, Anne, 1955-
    New York / Anne Welsbacher.
    p. cm. -- (United States)
    Includes index.
    Summary: Surveys the people, geography, and history of the Empire State.
    ISBN 1-56239-891-1
    1. New York (state)--Juvenile literature. [1. New York (State)] I. Title. II.
    Series: United States (Series)
    F119.3.W45 1998
    974.7--dc21   97-34110
                                                 CIP
                                                 AC

Contents

Welcome to New York

New York is home to the largest city in the United States—New York City! It is the business center of America. The city is also known for its tall buildings, theaters, and museums. People from all over the world visit New York City.

New York has small towns and natural wonders. The famous Niagara Falls is in northwestern New York. Lakes, forests, and mountains also cover the state.

New York is a big part of United States history. President George Washington said New York would become the center of an American **empire**. That's why New York is called the Empire State.

The world-famous Niagara Falls

Fast Facts

New York is one of the original 13 colonies

NEW YORK

Capital
Albany (101,082 people)
Area
47,379 square miles
(122,711 sq km)
Population
18,044,505 people
Rank: 2nd
Statehood
July 26, 1788
(11th state admitted)
Principal rivers
Hudson River
St. Lawrence River
Highest point
Mount Marcy;
5,344 feet (1,629 m)
Largest city
New York (7,322,564 people)
Motto
Excelsior
(Ever upward)
Song
"I Love New York"
Famous People
Woody Allen, George Gershwin,
John Jay, John D. Rockefeller,
Franklin D. Roosevelt, Theodore
Roosevelt

*S*tate Flag

*B*luebird

*R*ose

*S*ugar Maple

About New York

The Empire State

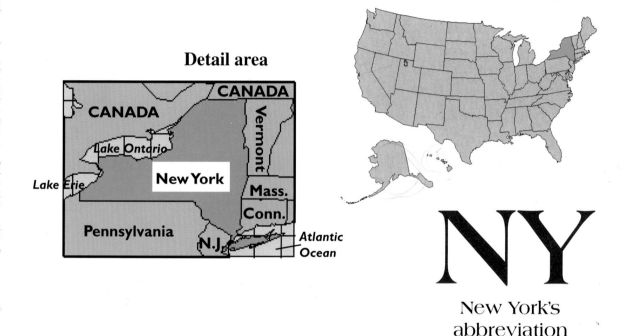

Detail area

CANADA

CANADA

Lake Ontario

Lake Erie

New York

Vermont

Mass.

Conn.

Pennsylvania

N.J.

Atlantic Ocean

NY

New York's
abbreviation

Borders: west (Canada, Lake Ontario, Lake Erie), north
(Canada), east (Vermont, Massachusetts, Connecticut),
south (Atlantic Ocean, New Jersey, Pennsylvania)

Nature's Treasures

New York has many lakes and rivers. There are also waterfalls and fast-moving waters called rapids. Because they move so fast, their power is used to run machines!

New York's land has lead, talc, and zinc. In some mountains are stones called garnets. They are used in jewelry and watches. The soil also holds sand, gravel, and clay, used to make cement.

The weather in New York is different around the state. Winters are below freezing in the mountains but mild in New York City. More rain falls in the mountains than in the city, too. And some places, like Buffalo, get more snow than most other big cities in the country!

Opposite page:
The Erie Canal

Beginnings

About 10,000 years ago, Native Americans lived in the area now called New York. By the 1300s, two big tribes called the Algonquian and Iroquois were in New York. They often fought with each other. Later they made peace and worked together.

In 1776, New York and other **colonies** signed a paper called the Declaration of Independence. The paper said the colonies were a new country. The 13 colonies fought and won the Revolutionary War against England. They became the United States of America. In 1788, New York became the 11th state.

In the early 1800s, New York built the Erie **Canal**. Now steamboats could carry goods from the Great Lakes and Buffalo to New York City. Railroads and roads were built, too. New York became the business center of America.

More **immigrants** came to New York. As they reached New York City, a big statue on Liberty Island welcomed them. Today, the Statue of Liberty remains a **symbol** of freedom for all Americans.

In the mid-1800s, nearly half a million men from New York fought against slavery in the Civil War. Many New York women spoke out against slavery. They also spoke for a woman's right to vote and to own things. This was known as the suffragist movement.

After the war, new machines were **invented**. They helped the state become a great maker of goods like clothing, shoes, and books.

The 20th century brought more immigrants and business. Harbors were improved, and airports were built. New York's towns and cities grew. Today, New York remains a state rich in business, nature, and peoples.

Immigrants in New York City

1300s to 1700s

Early Times, Early Battles

 1300s: Algonquian and Iroquois people live in the area now called New York.

 1600s: Settlers arrive from the Netherlands, England, and other countries.

 1689 to 1763: England and France fight in four big wars called the **French and Indian Wars**. England defeats France in 1763.

New York

1300s to 1700s

1788 to 1880s

A Doorway for All People

 1788: New York becomes the 11th state.

 1848: The first big women's rights meeting is held in Seneca Falls, New York.

 1880s: **Immigrants** from China, Eastern Europe, and Italy join earlier immigrants from Ireland and Germany.

New York

1788 to 1880s

1888 to Today

War and Peace

1888: The Kodak camera is **invented** in Rochester, New York.

1917: More people from New York than from any other state fight in World War I and, later, in World War II.

1939-40: The World's Fair is held in New York City.

1946: New York City is selected as the home for the **United Nations**. The building is finished in 1952.

1989: David Dinkins becomes the first African-American mayor of New York City.

New York

1888 to Today

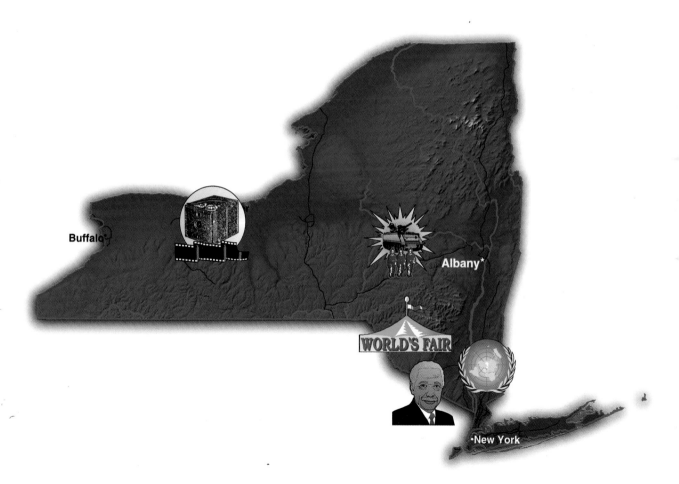

Buffalo

Albany

WORLD'S FAIR

New York

New York's People

There are over 18 million people in New York. Only the big state of California has more people. About seven million New Yorkers live in New York City. People of nearly every faith, race, and national background live in the state.

Actor Tom Cruise is from Syracuse. Alex Haley, who wrote *Roots*, was born in Ithaca. L. Frank Baum, who wrote *The Wonderful Wizard of Oz*, was from Chittenango. Maurice Sendak is from Brooklyn. He wrote *Where the Wild Things Are* and draws pictures for many children's books.

Basketball player Kareem Abdul-Jabbar is from New York City. Dodger pitcher Sandy Koufax and Yankee hitter Lou Gehrig were New Yorkers, too.

Woody Allen and Spike Lee, two moviemakers, and Shirley Chisholm were born in Brooklyn. Chisholm was the first African-American congresswoman.

Songwriter George Gershwin and Bella Abzug, who spoke for women's rights, were born in New York City.

Sojourner Truth was born a slave in Kingston, New York. She spoke against racism and for women's rights. President Franklin D. Roosevelt was also from New York, near Hyde Park.

Franklin D. Roosevelt

Sojourner Truth

Maurice Sendak

New York's Cities

New York City is the largest city in the state. It also is the state's largest **seaport.** Goods are shipped to and from countries all over the world.

Because it has so many businesses and makes so many things, New York City is the business center of America. The city has five **boroughs**. They are Manhattan, the Bronx, Queens, Brooklyn, and Staten Island.

The next largest city is Buffalo, a **port** city on Lake Erie. It is known as a railroad center where many goods are shipped to and from the Great

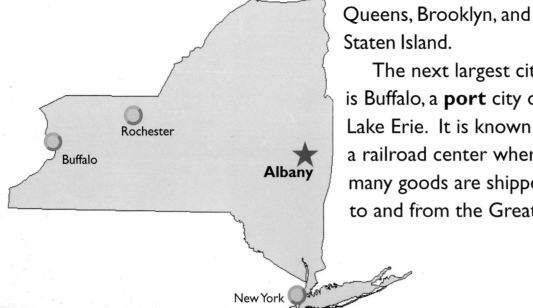

Rochester

Buffalo

Albany

New York

Lakes. The city also has many factories that make goods like steel, flour, and furniture.

Rochester is the third largest city. Near Lake Ontario, this **port** city also ships many kinds of goods to and from other states. The city is home to the Eastman Kodak Company, which makes cameras and film.

Albany is the capital of New York. It has many government buildings. Because it is on the Hudson River, Albany also is an inland **seaport**. It ships goods to Buffalo through the Erie Canal. The city's factories make things like paper, machine tools, and metal products.

The tall buildings of New York City

New York's Land

New York's land is divided into 10 areas. The Adirondack region is known for its beautiful mountains, valleys, and lakes. Lake Placid is in this region. Mount Marcy, the highest point in the state, towers over the area.

In the small Champlain Valley region are many lakes that make for fun vacations.

The St. Lawrence Valley has many islands, valleys, and rivers. The Lake Plains region stretches along the western part of the state. This area borders Lake Ontario

and Lake Erie. They are joined by the Niagara River. Halfway along the river is the famous Niagara Falls. This region also has the Erie Canal.

The Hudson Valley and Mohawk Valley regions are filled with rich farmland, and many rivers and valleys.

The Catskill Mountain and Taconic Mountain regions are split by the Hudson Valley region. These two mountain regions are filled with lakes and resorts for summer vacations.

The Coastal Plain region in southeastern New York spreads across the islands of New York City. This area has many sandy and rocky beaches.

The Allegheny Plateau is the largest region in New York. This area is known for the Finger Lakes and dairy farms.

The Finger Lakes

New York at Play

When it comes to having fun, nothing beats the "Fun City" of New York. On a street called Broadway, there are many plays and **musicals**. The city also has many places to shop, see art, and listen to music.

The city's Central Park has walking and bike paths, a lake, a small zoo, playgrounds, and an ice skating rink. The Bronx Zoo is in northern New York City. Every fall, runners run 26.2 miles (42 km) through the five **boroughs** for the New York **Marathon**.

New York City's baseball fans can watch the Yankees and Mets. The Yankees have won more championships than any other pro sports team.

The city's football fans can enjoy the Giants and the Jets. There's also a pro hockey team, the Rangers, and a pro basketball team, the Knicks. Uniondale, on Long Island, is home to pro hockey's New York Islanders.

In Buffalo are pro hockey's Sabres, and pro football's Bills. North of Buffalo, people can view the beautiful Niagara Falls.

Lake Placid is in the Adirondack Mountains. People swim in the summer and ski or watch bobsled races in the winter. The Winter Olympic Games have been held in Lake Placid, too.

Central Park, New York City

New York at Work

Many New Yorkers are doctors, nurses, or lawyers. Others sell things. Some work in **advertising**.

New Yorkers teach school and work in banks. Many people work on Wall Street. Here they buy and sell **stocks**. New Yorkers also work in factories.

New York farmers raise dairy cows to produce milk. They make maple syrup from tree sap. They also grow apples, cherries, and sweet corn.

Some New Yorkers catch perch and walleye from the Great Lakes. Others catch clams, lobsters, and oysters from the Atlantic Ocean. They sell their catch to grocery stores.

Opposite page: An illustration of the New York Stock Exchange

Fun Facts

•New York City has more bridges—2,100—than any other city in the country.

•"Uncle Sam" was born in Troy, New York. In the 1800s, a man in Troy named Samuel Wilson had a job putting meat in boxes to ship to other places. He sent many boxes of meat to soldiers fighting in the War of 1812. The boxes were marked "U.S." for United States. But because the country was so new, not everybody knew what U.S. stood for. They asked Wilson what U.S. meant, and he joked that it stood for Uncle Sam.

•New York City's World Trade Center, which has two big buildings, is so big it has two postal zip codes!

•The first escalator, or moving stairs, was made by a company in New York City in 1899.

•The teddy bear is named after New Yorker Theodore Roosevelt, who was president of the United States.

- The world's biggest theater is Radio City Music Hall in New York City.
- The man who built the Statue of Liberty used his mother as a model for the project.
- Smith Brothers cough drops were **invented** by two New York brothers named William Wallace Smith and Andrew Smith.
- The Dutch people who first came to New York brought new foods with them. They brought a cabbage salad we call coleslaw. And they brought fried cakes we call doughnuts.

The Statue of Liberty is so big that it can be seen from miles away.

Glossary

Advertising: the pictures and words on TV, billboards, and other places that show things, like cars or candy or toys, and try to talk people into buying them.

Borough: a part of a city.

Canal: a river made by people.

Colony: a place owned by another country.

Empire: a big and strong country that leads or rules other lands.

French and Indian Wars: four big wars fought over New York lands between England and France; some tribes of Native Americans (sometimes called Indians) fought on the side of England, while others fought on the side of France.

Immigrant: a person who moves to a country from another country.

Invent: to create something for the first time.

Marathon: a full marathon is a race, first run in the Olympics in ancient Greece, that is always 26.2 miles (42 km) long.

Musical: a play with songs and dancing.

Port: a city or town with a harbor.

Seaport: a city or town with a harbor that ships can reach from the sea.

Stock: the shares in a company that have value.

Symbol: something that stands for something else; the Statue of Liberty is a symbol of freedom.

United Nations: a place in New York City where people from many countries meet to try to bring peace to the world. The UN was founded after World War II.

Internet Sites

New York State
http://www.cybervillage.com/
A colorful and well-designed Web site that includes Marketplace, Entertainment, Education, Tourism, Community Services, and much more. Very interactive.

Our Home Town
http://www.our-hometown.com/
Our Hometown provides an internet home page with community information and local news for almost 100 towns and villages in the Western New York counties of Genesee, Livingston, Monroe, Ontario, Orleans, and Wayne.

Junior Achievement of New York
http://www.jany.org/
They're educating, motivating and inspiring over 100,000 students in New York City and Long Island. This Web site is very kid oriented, colorful and interactive. Check it out!

These sites are subject to change. Go to your favorite search engine and type in New York for more sites.

PASS IT ON

Tell Others Something Special About Your State

To educate readers around the country, pass on interesting tips, places to see, history, and little known facts about the state you live in. We want to hear from you!

To get posted on ABDO & Daughters Web site, E-mail us at "mystate@abdopub.com"

Index